THE SHADE
OF DEATH

TremA
THE EARTH
LORD

*With special thanks to Cherith Baldry*

*For Charlie Andrew Mills*

www.beastquest.co.uk

ORCHARD BOOKS
338 Euston Road, London NW1 3BH
*Orchard Books Australia*
Level 17/207 Kent St, Sydney, NSW 2000

A Paperback Original
First published in Great Britain in 2009

A CIP catalogue record for this book is available from
the British Library.

ISBN 978 1 40830 441 9

10

Printed in Great Britain by CPI Group (UK) Ltd, Croydon, CR0 4YY

The paper and board used in this paperback are natural recyclable
products made from wood grown in sustainable forests. The
manufacturing processes conform to the environmental regulations of
the country of origin.

Orchard Books is a division of Hachette Children's Books,
an Hachette UK company

www.hachette.co.uk

# TremA
# THE EARTH
# LORD

## BY ADAM BLADE

ORCHARD

THE ICE
CASTLE

CRESCENT CAVE

FREESHOR

T

GWILDORIAN
PLAINS

FA

THE RAINBOW JUNGLE

Gwildor

GWILDORIAN OCEAN

'MLAND

FISHING
VILLAGE

ON

*Welcome to a new world...*

*Did you think you'd seen all the evil that existed? You're almost as foolish as Tom! He may have conquered Wizard Malvel, but fresh challenges await him. He must travel far and leave behind everything he knows and loves. Why? Because he has six Beasts to defeat in a kingdom he can't even call home.*

*Will his heart be in it? Or will Tom turn his back on this latest Quest? Little does he know, but he has close ties to the people here. And a new enemy determined to ruin him. Can you guess who that enemy is...?*

*Read on to see how your hero fares.*

*Velmal*

# PROLOGUE

The full moon shed a cold light over the plains of Gwildor. A chill wind bent the grass and rustled the leaves.

The moonlight picked out the dark figure of a man, scuttling from one patch of shadow to the next. His hair and beard were ragged; he wore rough woollen trousers and a jerkin fastened at the waist with a rope, through which a spade was tucked.

He glanced furtively over his shoulder, as if afraid he was being followed.

At last the man halted in a spot where a few sharp stones poked through the grass. "This'll do," he muttered, with another swift look around. He let out a hoarse chuckle.

"You're a fine fellow, Ally," he mumbled to himself. "And soon you'll be rich!"

Ally pulled out the spade and began to dig, slowly at first, then faster as sweat plastered his hair to his forehead and dark stains spread on his tunic. He threw the earth aside as he dug deeper into the ground.

As Ally bent over the spade, his jerkin gaped open and a soft leather roll fell to the ground. Muttering a curse, Ally threw the spade aside and grabbed the roll. He started to thrust it inside his jerkin again, then paused.

"My treasure will look even more beautiful by the light of the moon," he murmured.

Smiling to himself, Ally unfurled the leather roll to reveal a set of tiny silver skulls strung on a chain. He held it up to see it glitter in the moonlight.

"You're mine, now. I'm sure your past owner will never miss you!" he said, laughing.

Ally's smile faded as a cold wind whistled around him, and he cast a nervous glance all around. He could see nothing but the empty plain, and some cattle grazing in the distance, but he still couldn't push away the feeling that he was being watched.

"I won't take any chances," he promised himself. "I'll bury my treasure here until it's safe to come back and collect it."

Carefully, he put the stolen silver skulls back inside the leather roll and set it down beside the hole. Then he dug with his spade again,

leaning further and further into the
hiding place he was making.

Suddenly, the ground beneath
Ally's spade seemed to shift. Long
cracks zig-zagged out from the hole.
Ally felt the earth shift underneath
his feet; soil erupted into the air. He
let out a cry of terror as he was
thrown to the ground.

All the breath was driven out of
Ally's body. Gasping, he heaved
himself up onto his elbows. His face
was set in a fierce scowl as he looked
to see what was happening.

His eyes bulged with terror. He
scrambled backwards, screaming, as
an enormous, slimy creature burst
out of the hole. A row of green
jewels on its head glowed against
the night sky.

The creature opened its mouth and

let out a howl of victory. Rows and
rows of razor-sharp teeth glistened
in the moonlight. It pulled the rest
of its body out of the hole and darted
across the ground towards Ally. He
heard the disgusting slurp of slime
as it bore down on him, its long body
rippling with muscle as its clawed
legs skimmed the ground.

The thief let out another yell of terror. Stumbling to his feet, he snatched up the leather roll and tried to run, but a jet of slime wrapped itself around his ankles. The slime dripped down, glowing green in the light of the jewels on the monster's head. Ally fought to regain his balance, but his feet slipped and he fell. More slime coated him and stuck him to the ground.

With a desperate struggle, Ally turned over on his back. The huge creature towered over him. Its vast mouth gaped open and began to descend. A hoarse cry escaped Ally as the moonlight was blotted out.

His career as a thief was over...

# CHAPTER ONE

# A NEW BEAST

Tom and Elenna rode Storm down
the mountain path. Though they had
left the snowfields behind, and the
hillsides were covered with heather
and gorse bushes, snow and ice still
gathered in the hollows.

Tom was sitting behind Elenna.
His injured hand still throbbed with
pain, and he couldn't hold the reins
to guide the stallion through the

treacherous patches of ice. So far, they had freed four Gwildorian Beasts from the spell of the evil wizard Velmal. The first Beast, Krabb, had caused Tom's injury with one of his giant pincers, and the green poison had been spreading through his hand ever since. But Tom had not let this stop him, and he and Elenna had managed to free Hawkite, Rokk, and Koldo as well.

Tom tried not to think about the threat Velmal had made after the battle with Koldo, the arctic warrior.

*"The next Quest will be your last,"* Velmal had said. *"None of you will leave Gwildor alive."*

Tom straightened his back and rested his hand on the hilt of his sword. *While there's blood in my veins, I'll go on fighting Velmal.*

Elenna glanced back at him, her eyes sparkling. "Are you ready for the next challenge?" she asked, almost as if she guessed what he had been thinking.

"Ready," he grinned. *Maybe I can help Freya, too,* he added to himself. *I must free her from Velmal's evil.*

Tom felt a strange connection to Freya, Mistress of the Beasts, but he couldn't understand why. Velmal's spell had made her almost as evil as the dark wizard himself.

The sun shone brightly from a pale blue sky. Its dazzling rays reflected from a patch of ice, so that Tom and Elenna had to squint their eyes against the glare.

"Everything's so much brighter here in Gwildor, compared to our home in Avantia," Elenna said. "Even Silver has to watch where he's putting his paws."

The glare made Tom's eyes water, and he had to blink to see the wolf padding carefully forward, his snout raised alertly to sniff out the track. Raising a hand to wipe his stinging eyes, Tom bit back a cry of pain as his salty tears trickled onto his poisoned wound. His hand was red and swollen, and it hurt to move it. Tom was so grateful that Elenna had not noticed how bad it was. So far.

*I can't let anything stop me on this Quest,* he thought. *Not even an injured hand.*

Gradually the path became less steep, giving way to broad grasslands. A warm, gentle wind welcomed Tom and Elenna as the plains of Gwildor opened out in front of them. The long grasses shone golden and rolled like the waves of the sea, dancing in the breeze.

Elenna slid down from Storm's back. "It's so beautiful!"

"It certainly is," Tom said, jumping down to Elenna's side. "But we can't stand here all day. We must find the next Beast, and the prize that will help us free it."

Elenna nodded, her face set in determination. "You're right. There's no time to lose."

Tom pulled the Amulet of Avantia from around his neck and turned it over to reveal the map of Gwildor etched into the metal. With Elenna peering over his shoulder, he watched as a single path appeared on the map.

"That's odd," Tom said, frowning. "Usually two paths appear."

"That must mean the prize and the Beast are close together," Elenna murmured.

Tom examined the amulet more closely. A cold prickle of uneasiness crept down his spine as he spotted the name of the Beast etched at the end of the path.

"Trema…" he murmured. *I wonder what form you will take…*

He gazed out across the plain in the direction the map was telling them to go. Shading his forehead with one hand, he screwed up his eyes against the sunlight, wishing that he still had the keen sight that he had won from the golden armour of Avantia.

"Looks like houses over there," he said. "I'm surprised Velmal will let us go near more people. Not after we freed the Beast the villagers had captured, and turned him back to being good again. That's not part of Velmal's plan!"

Elenna laughed. "Indeed. I don't suppose he wants his people to know that there's a hero in his kingdom!"

Tom couldn't share his friend's laughter. His uneasiness deepened as he thought about what was waiting for them on the plains. This could be the deadliest mission of all.

*But we won't turn back,* he told himself. *Whatever the dangers are, we'll face them together.*

Tom took a last look at the map and hung the amulet around his neck again. "We have to go where the map leads," he said. "And there's no time to waste!"

# CHAPTER TWO

# A PUZZLE ON THE PLAINS

Now that Tom and Elenna had left the steep mountain path, their journey was easier. Tom was able to manage Storm again, with Elenna riding behind.

"This is such a beautiful kingdom!" she exclaimed, gazing around at the rolling plains. "I can't believe that there's an evil here worse than Malvel's."

"I know what you mean," Tom agreed. A chill ran through him, in spite of the bright sunlight and warm breeze. They had already completed four Quests in this kingdom, but there were still two more prizes to win – and Tom knew that Velmal was evil, through and through.

Soon Tom began to spot cows dotted across the plain. They kept their distance from Tom and Elenna, though they raised their heads to watch them riding by. Their jaws moved from side to side as they lazily chewed grass.

Silver let out a teasing bark as he bounded ahead, his plumy tail waving. The cows edged away from him, though the wolf wasn't chasing them.

"He knows better than to go near

the cattle," Elenna said. "But he can't resist having some fun!"

Storm ignored the cows altogether, plodding obediently along their path. Tom leant forward to pat his glossy black neck. *Storm never loses sight of our Quest!*

Slowly, more cows appeared, until Tom and Elenna were riding through the middle of a herd. Elenna called Silver back to pad along beside the horse.

Tom examined the cattle as they fed peacefully, their tails flicking lazily to scare away flies. "Strange, isn't it?" he said to Elenna. "*We* know there's a Beast around here somewhere, so why aren't the cows spooked?"

He heard Elenna release a hiss of breath from between her teeth.

"You're right!" she exclaimed.

"None of these animals seem worried or scared at all."

"All of our Quests have shown us that no animal likes to be around a Beast," Tom added, shaking his head in confusion. Lifting the amulet, he took another look at the map on the back. "We're still heading in the right direction," he said. "And the Beast can't be far off."

"Could the Beast be a shape-shifter?" Elenna suggested.

"Yes, or invisible." Tom gazed out at the herd again with narrowed eyes. He didn't like the idea of a Beast watching them when they couldn't see it. "There's only one way to find out," he said, squaring his shoulders. "We must hurry onwards!"

As they rode on, Tom could make out farm buildings, and a town just beyond them. "We're almost there. Let's rest and take another look at the map before we go on."

Tom heaved himself out of the saddle, but as he leapt to the ground he stumbled and had to put out his hands to break his fall. Pain tore through his injured hand. He let out a cry and pulled his hand protectively against his chest. His head swam as the pangs stabbed up his arm.

"Tom?" Elenna's voice was anxious. She jumped down beside him and gently prised his hand away from his body. "Tom," she gasped. "You never told me it was as bad as this!"

Tom stared at his hand. He had tried to ignore it by tucking it inside his jerkin. Now he saw that it was more swollen than ever, with streaks of red creeping up his arm. The puncture wounds where Krabb's claw had pierced him were crusted with purple scabs, and the skin was beginning to split.

"Have you any herbs left?" he asked Elenna, his voice faint and quivering in spite of his efforts to steady it.

Elenna found her pouch, fastened to Storm's saddle, and rummaged inside it. She turned away, shaking her head. "We've used the last of it. I'm sorry, Tom."

Tom felt his legs grow weaker. He sank to the ground, leaning back against Silver, who braced himself, whining anxiously. He heard Storm stamping his hooves in the grass, whinnying with concern.

*I can't give way now,* he thought desperately. *I have a Beast to fight.* But his body wouldn't obey him when he tried to scramble to his feet again.

Elenna started to climb into Storm's saddle. "I'm going to find some help," she said. "I'll be back as quickly as I can."

"No, Elenna," Tom groaned. "I need you here."

Dark clouds of pain swirled around Tom and he struggled to stay conscious. Through blurred eyes he saw Elenna looking down at him, worry etched across her face.

*I'll be fine,* Tom wanted to reassure her, but he could not speak.

It would be easy to rest in the dark that was gathering around him, free from pain. But Tom knew that if he slept now, it would all be over.

He forced his eyes open. *Must. Stay. Awake.*

Then he saw Elenna throw her hands up towards the sky. "Aduro, we need your help!" she called out desperately.

The air glittered. Tom caught his breath, beginning to hope again. Would the good wizard of Avantia really be able to appear and help them?

A purple glow appeared in the air. A tall, imposing figure began to form in front of Tom and Elenna. Tom stared in disbelief at the long, flame-red hair and flowing robes, the jutting nose and sneering expression, and the two curved axe-heads at the top of the staff gripped in the figure's hand.

*I don't believe this! I must be dreaming!*

But Elenna's cry of terror told Tom that this was no trick of the eye. This was real.

Velmal had appeared before them!

# CHAPTER THREE

# VELMAL'S RIDDLE

Tom peered up at Velmal through a haze of pain, meeting his cold, mocking eyes. Elenna moved to her friend's side and stood facing up to the evil wizard, anger and defiance in her expression.

"What do you want, Velmal?" she demanded. "You're a coward for appearing now, when Tom cannot defend himself."

The wizard let out a snort of contempt. "It's not as if the boy's at death's door," he sneered, fixing his glittering eyes on Tom. "More's the pity."

"Tell me how I can help him," she demanded.

Tom didn't think she really expected an answer from Velmal, but the wizard smiled thinly and spoke. *"Ichor Ofkin, Kin ichor,*

Red to red, life from death."

"What does that mean?" Elenna shouted.

The evil wizard just went on repeating his mysterious words, his voice rising to a chant. He flung his head back and raised his arms in the air, flourishing his staff.

Tom stared in amazement as fire sprang around Velmal's feet, licking up his robes but not burning them. The smoke swirled around the wizard and his figure slowly faded. The purple glow died. The riddle Velmal was chanting lasted a moment more before it, too, faded away.

Nothing was left of Velmal except for a few smouldering embers of charcoal. Immediately, Elenna ran to Storm's side, snatching the water bottle that hung on his saddle.

Tom groaned with pain as he watched his friend pour a few drops of their precious water on the charcoal and mix it to a paste.

"What are you doing?" he asked.

Elenna scooped up some of the paste and pressed it against Tom's poisoned wound. "Velmal didn't mean to help us, but he has," she explained. "One of my uncles taught me this trick when I fell into some poison ivy. Charcoal helps to draw out poison!"

Fumes from the charcoal filled Tom's nostrils. His senses swam; he felt as if the pain in his hand was easing. Gradually his eyelids drooped. At last, he gave in to the exhaustion that was sweeping over him. The last thing he saw was Elenna's anxious face gazing down at him. Then darkness enveloped him...

Tom opened his eyes to see mist swirling across the plain. The grey light of dawn was all around him. Elenna had draped a blanket over his body and put a saddlebag under his head.

Beside him she was sleeping, curled

up in another blanket, with Silver
huddled at her side. Half-hidden by
the mist, Storm was cropping the
grass, his contented snorts sounding
loud in the chilly morning air.

Tom sat up and saw that Elenna had bound the charcoal poultice to his hand with a bandage. The pain had faded to a dull ache. Tom carefully peeled the bandage away and saw that his hand looked much better. It wasn't as swollen and the red streaks had disappeared. The split in his skin looked as if it was healing.

Relief flooded through him. He leapt to his feet, waking Silver, who raised his head and let out a bark of greeting. That was enough to wake Elenna. As soon as she saw Tom, she scrambled up and peered at his injured hand.

"The charcoal worked!" she exclaimed, throwing her arms around him.

Tom smiled and gently released himself. "What would I do without you?" he asked. "You may have just saved my life. Thank you. I wish I could thank your uncle, too!"

"I'm just glad you're OK," Elenna exclaimed. Her cheeks were pink with embarrassment. "I've wrapped up the rest of the charcoal, so we can use it again if your hand gets worse."

"Good idea." Tom paused, recalling

the pain and confusion of the previous evening. He pictured Velmal, his arms raised to the sky, chanting words that seemed to have no meaning. "Did I dream Velmal and his riddle?" he asked. "Or did that really happen?"

Elenna's smile faded. "Yes, it really happened."

"Do you remember what he said?"

Elenna frowned thoughtfully, and then recited, *"Ichor Ofkin, Kin ichor,*

Red to red, life from death."

*"Ichor Ofkin*… I wonder what it means," Tom said.

"I've no idea," Elenna said, shaking her head in bewilderment.

For a moment Tom stood still, letting the mystical words run through his mind. Then he shook his head, dismissing the puzzle. "I'm sure Velmal didn't recite it to help us," he told Elenna. "Come on. We have got to carry on with our Quest."

Silver let out an approving howl, and ran a few paces towards the town, as if he was trying to tell Tom and Elenna to hurry up.

"Silver's right," Tom said as Elenna rolled up the blankets and fastened them to Storm's saddle. "The map was leading us to that settlement. That's where we have to go!"

# CHAPTER FOUR

# A HARD BARGAIN

Tom and Elenna led Storm along a muddy road, until at last they came to the town square. On one side, Tom spotted a junk shop, with pots and pans, brooms and hunting spears arranged on the ground in front of it. While Tom watched, the shopkeeper came out and dumped a stack of earthenware bowls beside the door, and went back inside.

On the other side of the square, traders were setting out their goods on market stalls. Tom could see heaped up piles of fruit, polished bowls of copper and brass, and bales of wool and linen, all in the bright colours of Gwildor. The first customers of the day were hurrying into the square, greeting each other cheerfully,

carrying baskets to carry their wares.

Elenna pulled at Tom's sleeve.
"Look! There's a stall selling bread.
I'm so hungry!"

"So am I," Tom said. He breathed in
the delicious smell of warm loaves
just out of the oven. It made him feel
hungrier than ever. "But we've no
money."

Elenna led the way over to the stall, looking longingly at the warm bread. As the stall-holder was stacking up his loaves; Tom noticed a red, angry-looking burn on one of his hands.

"It looks as if he had an accident with his oven," he murmured to Elenna.

"Yes." Elenna's eyes suddenly brightened. "And I know what to do!"

Tom watched as his friend walked up to the stall-holder. Knowing Elenna, she had some clever plan up her sleeve!

"Good morning," Elenna said as she reached the stall. "That's a nasty burn you've got there."

The man glanced at his hand. "I know. It's my own fault. I was too clumsy getting the loaves out of the oven this morning."

"I've got a charcoal poultice that might help you," Elenna suggested. "I'll give it to you in exchange for a loaf."

The stall-holder smiled. "That might be the best bargain I'll make all day."

Elenna went back to Storm and fetched some of the charcoal paste. She spread it over the burn on the stall-holder's hand; he gave her a handkerchief to bind it in place.

"That feels better already," the stall-holder said. "A thousand thanks, young mistress. Here's your bread." He picked out the biggest loaf from the stack and handed it to Elenna.

"Thank you." Elenna carried the loaf back to Tom. "Here you are. Breakfast."

"Well done!" Tom said admiringly. "I'd never have thought of that."

Elenna tore the loaf into three pieces. She gave one piece to Tom, and one to Silver. The wolf let out a grateful yelp, while Storm shook his bridle as he bent his head to eat some of the grass from a patch of lawn in the square.

"This is delicious!" Tom mumbled as he stuffed the steaming chunks into his mouth.

"It's not the biggest meal we've ever had," Elenna said, gulping down a mouthful. "But it will do for now."

As Tom ate his bread he looked back across the square towards the junk shop. Something seemed to be drawing him to it. When he glanced at the back of the amulet, a line appeared pointing in that direction.

"I think that's where the next prize must be," he whispered to Elenna, pointing towards the shop.

Tom led Storm across the square. Elenna walked beside him with Silver at her heels. Outside the shop, Tom tied Storm to an iron post.

"Stay, Silver," Elenna told her animal friend. "We won't be long."

The wolf flopped to the ground beside the stallion's hooves and rested his head on his paws.

Tom pushed open the door to enter the shop, brushing aside a cobweb that hung from the door frame. Dust lay thick on the floor. Inside, the shop was dimly lit. The shopkeeper was perched on a stool at the far side, poring over a leather-bound book. He was a shrunken old man with white hair and a wispy beard. As Tom and

Elenna entered, he looked up and peered at them over the top of half-moon glasses. He didn't speak; after a moment he went back to his book.

Tom and Elenna looked around the shop. The shopkeeper continued to ignore them. Tom wondered what the prize would be. He gazed up at a stuffed bull's head mounted on the wall, with a string of fishing hooks hanging from its horns. He picked up a tarnished silver bowl and put it down again.

*I'm sure when I find the prize I'll feel something to tell me I'm right.*

Elenna was turning over the items in a basket of broken jewellery, her expression doubtful as she examined each one and discarded it.

Tom moved further into the shop, among dusty chests and cupboards. Perhaps he had been wrong to think that the prize could be hidden in this dingy little shop.

"Let's go," he said to Elenna.

"There's nothing here."

As he was turning towards the door, he noticed a dresser with a hand mirror lying on one of the shelves, mixed up with a tangle of old scarves and belts. The back of the mirror was encrusted with glittering stones that glinted with an eerie light.

Tom glanced at Elenna. She was looking at the mirror as well. "Do you think that could be the prize?" she asked in a low voice.

Crossing the shop, Tom disentangled the mirror and picked it up. As soon as he did so he felt a bolt of energy race down his arm.

"This is it!" he whispered to Elenna. "I'm sure it's the prize we've been looking for."

"How are we going to pay for it?" Elenna asked anxiously. "I don't think charcoal poultices will be enough this time!"

"I don't know," Tom replied. "But we have to have it," he murmured, half to himself. "And we can't tell the shopkeeper why. We'll just have to hope he's in a generous mood!"

Hesitantly Tom approached the shopkeeper, holding out the mirror. "Er... I'd like to borrow this," he began.

The shopkeeper looked up from his book. Even before he spoke, Tom could already see the laugh of scorn bubbling up inside the man's chest.

"*Borrow* it?" the shopkeeper began. "Do you think I'd stay in business if I lent my stock to every scruffy young lad who sets foot in my shop?"

"You can have this," Elenna said quickly, stepping up beside Tom. She held out her quiver of arrows.

Tom stared at Elenna in disbelief. *I can't believe she'd give up her arrows*, he thought. Elenna had never abandoned her weapons before.

"It's the horse or nothing," the shopkeeper said, peering out of the window at Storm. "He's fourteen hands high. I could get a good price for him if you don't come back!"

Tom didn't want to be parted from

his faithful stallion, but as he gazed out of the window he could see Storm patiently watching and waiting. He knew that his horse had always done whatever he could to help on each Quest. Perhaps Storm was ready to help again now?

"If that's the only way," Tom said slowly. He reached out and shook the shopkeeper's hand.

"If you don't bring the mirror back by the next rise of the moon, the horse is mine for good," the shopkeeper said.

Tom didn't like this deal, but what could he do? For the first time, he realised quite how much this Quest meant: enough to risk losing Storm.

# CHAPTER FIVE

# SILVER IN DANGER

The shopkeeper followed Tom and Elenna outside as they left the shop. He walked over to Storm and patted him on the brow. The stallion nodded his head showing that he understood, and blew warm breath out through his nose.

Tom examined the mirror in the morning sun, admiring how the stones glittered with a clear, icy light.

"I've never seen stones like these before," he said to the shopkeeper. "Their light seems...unusual."

The shopkeeper puffed his chest out proudly. "They're diamonds, and they're mined just outside our town," he announced, pointing down the street towards the plain. "They're very rare – this is the only place in Gwildor where you can find them."

A tingle of excitement ran through Tom, and he exchanged a glance with Elenna. "The Beast must be in the mine!" he whispered.

"Yes," Elenna replied. "The map was right: the Beast and the prize are very close together."

"Thank you for your help," Tom said to the shopkeeper. He unfastened Storm's saddlebag and slung it over his shoulder, sliding his other arm

through the straps of his shield. Then
he gave Storm's nose a farewell rub.
"We'll be back soon, Storm," he
promised.

With Elenna and Silver beside him,
Tom set off down the street in the
direction the shopkeeper had pointed.

"If we're going down a mine, we
wouldn't be able to take Storm with
us," he said. "He's probably better off
with the shopkeeper."

"I hope so." Elenna was looking
worried. "I wish we hadn't had to
bargain with him."

"There wasn't anything else we
could do," Tom reassured her. "And
we'll come back for him once we've
finished this part of our Quest."

He gave the mirror another glance
before he tucked it into the
saddlebag. "I've no idea how that's

going to help us against Trema!"
he said.

For now it could stay with the rest
of Freya's prizes that he had won so
far: the pearl, the ring, the scales and
the gloves.

Tom and Elenna left the town
behind and headed out across the
plain. They hadn't gone far when
Tom spotted something sticking up
out of the grass.

"Over there!" he said.

As they drew closer, they saw a
rickety wooden platform covering a
gaping hole in the ground. It creaked
faintly in the breeze. Silver sniffed at
the bottom of one of the planks and
let out a whine.

"This must be the mine shaft,"
Tom said.

Elenna gazed around doubtfully. "It

looks as if no one has been here for years."

"I'm not surprised," Tom replied. "The ground under our feet is probably hollow after all that mining."

Elenna looked alarmed. "Silver, come away from—" she began.

A loud rumble from under their feet interrupted her. Tom felt the ground shake as the noise grew louder and louder. Fear bubbled up inside him.

"What's happening?" Elenna cried.

A huge explosion shot out of the mine shaft: earth and stones fountained up into the air and rained down. Powering up from the depths of the earth came a huge monster! Slime oozed from its belly, glowing a sickly green in the light that shone from a line of jewels on the creature's head. The Beast fixed smouldering eyes on Tom in a threatening glare. Its long, slimy body was encased in a shiny blue shell, like a suit of armour. Reaching out from each side were numerous pairs of thin legs ending in razor-sharp claws.

"Trema," Tom gasped. "The Beast!"

As Tom stood frozen in horror, Trema's jaws opened to reveal rows of spiny teeth. He let out a roar; his back arched down and his open mouth closed over Silver.

"No!" Elenna screamed, vainly struggling across the mounds of loose soil and stones to reach the wolf. "Tom, help him!"

Tom sprang forward, drawing his sword, but the earth was shuddering under his feet and he fell. He could not regain his balance. He tried to crawl forward and reach Silver, but he wasn't fast enough.

Trema's jaws were gripping the back of Silver's neck. He lifted the wolf off the ground and Silver's paws flailed helplessly. He howled desperately.

The slug-like monster sank back into the mine shaft, dragging Silver with him. The hole collapsed after them, earth flowing down into it until Trema and the wolf had disappeared.

"No!" Elenna cried. "Silver!" She scrambled over to where the mine shaft had been, scrabbling in the loose earth. But the tunnel had caved in and there was no way for her to follow her animal friend.

She looked up, her face streaked with dirt. "Tom, we've got to do something!"

# CHAPTER SIX

# UNDER THE EARTH

Tom grabbed his saddlebag from where he had flung it on the ground. Frantically he scrabbled inside it for the mirror.

"Do you think Freya's latest prize will help?" Elenna asked.

"It might," said Tom. "It was sent to us for a reason. It's the only hope we have, if we want to rescue Silver."

As he pulled the mirror out of the bag, it caught the sunlight. Tom screwed up his eyes at the dazzling flash of light from the diamonds.

"That's it!" he exclaimed aloud.

"What are you doing?" Elenna asked. "How will that save Silver?"

"Watch," Tom told her.

Checking the position of the sun, he angled the mirror so that the light from the diamonds was reflected onto the ground where the Beast had disappeared. Where the jet of sunlight hit the ground, a tunnel began to appear. The earth burned away, leaving a gaping hole in the ground.

"Yes!" Tom yelled. "It works." He lowered the mirror and approached the edge of the hole, peering down into the darkness. The hole reached so far below ground that he couldn't see where it ended. Smoke curled away from the sides where the hole had been burnt, revealing twinkling shards of stone set in the earth.

"Tom, you're so clever!" Elenna said as she came to crouch beside him. "I'd never have thought of doing that."

Tom gave her a quick, encouraging grin. "We'll soon get Silver back," he promised. "Can you jump down there? We don't know how deep it goes."

Elenna nodded firmly. "I'll do whatever it takes."

Tom picked up his sword and shield and slung the saddlebag over his shoulder, stowing the mirror inside it. Then he and Elenna stood together at the mouth of the hole.

"I'll go first," Tom said, trying not to think of how deep the hole was, or what might be waiting for them at the bottom. "One, two, three!" Holding his arms close to his body, he leapt down into the darkness.

Tom felt virtually weightless as he fell. It seemed a long time before he landed heavily on a pile of soft soil, which broke his fall. The top of the hole, with its blue circle of sky, was far above his head.

Quickly Tom scrambled to one side, out of Elenna's way as she jumped down to join him. Together they climbed to their feet, brushing loose earth away. Tom flexed his arms and legs and patted his body to check that he wasn't injured.

"I'm fine," he said to Elenna. "How about you?"

Elenna was also checking herself for injuries. Then she nodded. "I'm all right. Let's—"

She broke off at the sound of drawn-out howling, echoing from the end of a long tunnel. "That's Silver!" she exclaimed. "Oh, let's hurry!"

Tom gripped his sword and held his shield to cover them both from any unexpected attacks as they ventured through the tunnel. The sides were smooth, daubed here and there with the slime from Trema's belly. Cracks in the tunnel roof let in thin streams of daylight.

"Trema must have made those cracks when he forced his way out of the ground," Tom said.

"It's a good thing he did," Elenna agreed. "Otherwise we'd be blind as moles!"

By the light of the distant sunshine, Tom and Elenna made their way cautiously through the tunnel.

"Now I understand why none of the cattle were spooked by the Beast," Tom said after a while. "Trema is so far underground that they don't know he's here."

Elenna nodded, shivering. "I don't like it down here. Look at those bones!"

Tom looked where she pointed and spotted rat skeletons embedded in the tunnel walls. A heap of white bones was lying on the ground beside the wall. Teeth were scattered around it, and a silver chain strung with tiny silver skulls was tangled among the bones.

"That must have been another of Trema's victims," Tom said. "Those bones look human to me." Shuddering at the thought, he added, "I think the Beast sucks the flesh off his victims' bones."

"Oh, Silver!" Elenna's voice shook. "I hope we're in time to save you!"

Another howl from the end of the tunnel told them that the silver wolf was still alive. In spite of the gloomy light, Tom and Elenna broke into a run.

Soon they burst out of the tunnel, into a huge cavern that opened from one of the old mine shafts. The walls were rough grey rock, glistening here and there where water dripped down. Light angled down from cracks in the earth far above their heads.

In the centre of the cavern, Trema was circling Silver, who struggled vainly to free himself from the slime that oozed from the Beast's belly. As Tom watched, a wave of slime rippled out from Trema, eddying around the wolf. Trema's muscles flexed as he moved closer to Silver, spreading even more slime that pulsed green in the light of the jewels on his head.

"See that glowing green slime," Tom exclaimed. "That must be how Velmal is enchanting the Beast. The colour green has shown us the weak spot of every Beast so far. If I can destroy the slime, I can release Trema from his evil spell."

Silver was snarling and snapping his jaws defiantly, his paws were stuck to the cavern floor, and he couldn't get near enough to bite the Beast.

Trema's mouth gaped, revealing his spiny teeth. He seemed to give an evil smile as he saw the wolf glued to the floor. His body reared up as if he was about to swoop down and devour his victim.

"Tom!" Elenna called. "There isn't time to work it out. We've got to rescue Silver!"

# CHAPTER SEVEN

# TREMA'S LAIR

Elenna unslung her bow from her
shoulder and plucked an arrow out
of her quiver.

The wolf was struggling to free
himself from the slime, but he was
too firmly trapped. The slime was like
glue; Silver couldn't run away from
the Beast, but he snarled and showed
his teeth as Trema loomed over him.

Tom let the saddlebag fall, raised his sword and raced across the cavern. As he ran, Elenna's arrows zipped past him, rebounding from Trema's shell. The Beast's head thrashed to and fro and he swivelled around to face Elenna. Tom slipped past unnoticed.

*Well done, Elenna!* Tom thought. *Keep him distracted.*

Leaping over Trema's tail, Tom drew close to Silver, making sure that he didn't tread in the slime.

"Don't worry, boy," he muttered. "I'll soon get you free."

Silver whined a welcome as Tom stooped down and swept his sword through the glowing green slime under the wolf's feet. Silver gave a tremendous heave and managed to pull himself free.

"Here, boy! Over here!" Elenna
shouted.

As Silver ran over to her, Trema
saw that the wolf was free. Swinging
around, he spotted Tom, and let out a
furious roar. Slime drooled from his
rows of sharp teeth.

"Come on! Fight!" Tom yelled.

Stepping forward, Tom swung his sword at Trema. But the Beast was swift, despite his long, clumsy body. He scuttled out of the way before Tom could land a blow. Tom followed him, but it was hard to get close without treading in the slime that oozed out of the Beast and made a sticky trap all around him.

Trema reared up, clutching at Tom with four of his front claws. Tom swung his shield up to defend himself, and the claws scraped over its surface. The blow jarred Tom's injured hand. He cried out, only just managing to hold onto his shield.

Then, one of Trema's legs reached around the shield and grabbed Tom by the ankle. Its touch was cold and slimy. Tom let out a yell of alarm as the Beast hauled him into the air, dangling him upside down. Then, with a flick, she flipped him upright.

Tom twisted in the Beast's grip, lashing out with his sword. But the blade bounced harmlessly off the Beast's shining blue shell. Trema's head hovered over Tom, his mouth gaping, ready to engulf him. Tom's heart thumped with fear. *Is this the end of my Quest?*

"Tom!" Elenna cried out. She was still shooting her arrows at the Beast, but they bounced off and fell to the ground. Silver bounded forward, letting out defiant yelps, but was unable to reach Tom because of the pool of slime surrounding Trema.

Desperately, Tom twisted his head around and sank his teeth into Trema's leg, wincing at the bitter taste. He shuddered as he heard the crack of the Beast's shell breaking.

Trema let out a high-pitched shriek and dropped Tom, who put out his arms to save himself. He landed on the cavern floor with a thud, his injured hand striking the ground.

He choked back a cry of pain and clambered stiffly to his feet. Trema had slumped to the floor, his injured leg twitching. But Tom knew he wouldn't stay like that for long. A minor wound wouldn't stop this fearsome Beast!

"Tom!" Elenna called, shooting another arrow from her bow. "Trema's shell is too thick. Swords and arrows aren't any use. We have to think of something!"

*The slime!* Tom thought. *That has to be the key to defeating Trema. But how can I use it?*

He swung his shield around as Trema scuttled towards him again, reaching out with his legs. Fending off the grabbing claws, Tom looked around. There didn't seem to be any kind of weapon in the cavern that he could use against the Beast. In desperation, Tom scrambled back for the saddlebag and brought his mirror out, angling it around the cave so that the reflection of light darted from spot to spot. *This has to help!* he thought. *Otherwise, why have I been given this prize?*

Suddenly, a thin column of smoke began to rise into the air. Peering closer, Tom could see that a spot on the cave wall was being burnt away by the reflected light from the mirror. The rock wall crumbled away to the ground, revealing a snow white patch of colour. Crystals sparkled in the dim light and Tom carefully put out a hand to the glimmering white cave wall. Holding his fingers to his mouth he tasted...

"Salt!" he cried.

As Trema's claws battered against his shield, a plan flashed into Tom's mind. "If I can lure Trema over to the wall, the salt could dry up his slime," he called to Elenna.

"It might work," Elenna shouted. "We've got to try!"

*Yes, it might work,* Tom thought, though a cold shiver of fear ran through him. *But the only way I can coax Trema over there is by using myself as bait.*

# CHAPTER EIGHT

# BURIED ALIVE!

"While there's blood in my veins, I'll risk everything to defeat this Beast!" he cried.

He scrambled backwards quickly towards the cavern wall and backed up against it, feeling the sparkling salt crystals scratch his skin. Then, bracing himself, he did something he had never done before in any other of his Beast Quests. He threw his sword aside.

"Tom! What are you doing?" Elenna cried as the blade clanged on the stone floor.

Tom didn't reply. He waited for Trema without a weapon, without anything to defend himself with. His heart pounded, but he kept his head high, facing the Beast.

Trema's jaws gaped in an evil smile. His belly oozed even more slime and the row of green jewels on his head sparkled joyously. He darted across the cavern floor towards Tom. Faster and faster he came.

Tom swung his shield around in front of him. Seeing it, Trema let out a roar of victory. *He doesn't think my shield will be any use*, Tom thought.

Tom waited, his muscles tense, for

Trema to get closer.

As Trema lunged towards him, his front legs raised and his claws slashing, Tom tried to dart to one side, but his foot slipped on Trema's slime. He stumbled and fell to one knee.

"Tom, no!" Elenna called out. Silver let out an anguished howl.

*I'm stuck!* Tom thought, his heart pounding as Trema loomed over him. Looking up, Tom saw a victorious glint in the Beast's eyes. As Trema opened his jaw a blast of foul air blew over Tom. He forced himself to meet the Beast's gaze as he came closer. *I have to escape,* Tom told himself, pulling his limbs from the slime. At the last moment he wrenched himself free and flung himself out of the Beast's path.

The Beast crashed into the wall. Crystals pierced his body and scattered across the ground under his tail. Trema's body seemed to stick to the salty wall and Tom watched, open mouthed, as the Beast's skin shrivelled tighter and tighter so that his eyes bulged; he threw his head back, letting out a wail of agony.

Tom stared, amazed, as Trema wriggled and thrashed. The green light in the jewels on his head slowly faded, and the jewels themselves crumbled to dust. The great Beast became still and, before Tom's amazed eyes, seemed to *sink* into the salty wall. Tom gasped as he saw that a thick crack had opened up, into which the Beast retreated. The salty wall fell in on itself, soon looking like it had never been disturbed. Tom listened for a moment, hearing the soft rumbling of Trema moving through the caves beyond. Free of Velmal's evil magic, the Beast had returned to protecting Gwildor's underworld.

Elenna raced across the cavern, with Silver at her heels. The wolf threw his head back and howled with triumph; the sound echoed around the cavern.

"Tom, that was wonderful!" Elenna cried. "You were so brave! I thought Trema was going to kill you."

"It was the only way I could see to defeat him," Tom replied.

Elenna's eyes sparkled and a wide grin spread over her face. "We've defeated another Beast. And we have Freya's prize."

"The shopkeeper still has Storm," Tom reminded her. "But we need to keep the mirror if we're to complete the rest of our Quest in Gwildor."

"We need something else to give the shopkeeper instead of the mirror," Elenna said. "But what?"

Tom spotted a huge diamond shining among the salt crystals on the cavern wall. Picking up his sword, he used the point to prise the diamond out. "This should be enough to pay him for the mirror *and* get Storm back," he said, grinning.

He retrieved Storm's saddlebag from where he had dropped it at the mouth of the tunnel, and stowed the diamond inside. Meanwhile, Elenna collected her spent arrows.

Just as they turned to go back through the tunnel the way they'd come, Tom heard a low rumbling coming from the other end of the tunnel, growing louder. He spun around to see a cloud of dust rolling along the passage. It billowed out into the cavern, choking him and stinging his eyes.

"Look!" Elenna exclaimed. "The tunnel's fallen in!"

# CHAPTER NINE

# THE GOLDEN ROPE

"Don't worry, we'll get out of here," said Tom. He wouldn't let them be trapped in the cavern. Not while there was a Quest to finish.

He looked up at the cavern roof. There! He could just see a sliver of light working its way into the cave from a distant crack. He angled the mirror, trying to catch whatever tiny amount of sunlight he could.

"We're a long way underground, Tom," said Elenna. "Even if you burn a hole in the roof with the mirror, we'll have to climb all the way to the top!"

"We'll find a way," Tom said, trying to sound confident. Clouds of dust surrounded them, specks dancing in the thin ray of sunlight, and he could still hear the sound of rumbling from the tunnel. But he refused to give up hope. There had to be a way out!

After moving the mirror several times, he managed to catch a jet of light and reflect it at the cavern roof near the crack. Smoke curled around the edge of the crack and slowly a bigger hole opened up. Tom and Elenna leapt back as soil cascaded down over them. Silver sprang away and stood shaking his pelt, growling softly.

Sunlight poured down from the hole in the cavern roof, far above their heads.

"So how shall we get up there?" Elenna asked, looking around for a solution.

She had hardly finished speaking when a thin golden rope fell down through the hole, and dangled in front of them, waiting for them to climb.

Elenna's eyes stretched wide with amazement. "Where did that come from?"

Tom stepped forward and touched the rope gently, then gave it a tug. It felt strong and firm. Glancing at Elenna, he murmured, "We have to trust it. It's our only way out. I'll carry Silver on my shoulders. You go first, and be ready to grab him when I get up there."

Elenna gave Silver's muzzle a swift rub. "Don't be afraid, boy. I'll see you at the top."

Silver whined softly in reply.

Carrying the saddlebag over her

shoulder, as well as her bow and arrows, Elenna gripped the rope and pulled herself up it. Tom watched as she disappeared through the hole in the roof. He was relieved that she had made it safely, but he couldn't help wondering what she had found outside. Then her head appeared again.

"The rope's tied to a rock!" she called. "I can't see who put it there."

"I'm coming up!" Tom replied. "Keep a lookout."

He knelt down and hauled Silver onto his shoulders. "Just keep still, boy," he muttered.

Standing up again, his back bowed under the weight of the wolf, Tom gripped the rope. Pain shot through his poisoned hand as he started to climb; he clenched his teeth on a yell of agony. He knew this was the only way to freedom.

*But who do we have to thank for the rope?* Tom wondered.

The hole in the roof seemed a long way away. Tom inched slowly upward, trying to ignore the pain in his hand. Silver lay across his shoulders; Tom could feel the wolf's breath warm in his ear.

Gradually Tom climbed up to the surface. As he popped his head out of the hole, Elenna leant down and grabbed Silver. Tom felt the wolf's hind paws scrabbling against his shoulders; then his weight vanished as Elenna strained to haul him up.

Tom was able to pull himself out of the hole. He collapsed on the ground, gasping for breath, waves of pain from his injured hand flooding over him.

He was still lying there when he heard the drumming of hooves. Looking up, Tom saw Storm come galloping across the plains, to halt beside him, snorting and pawing the ground.

"He must have escaped from the shopkeeper!" Elenna exclaimed.

Tom sat up, grinning. "Maybe he's

not always so well-behaved! We need
to keep the mirror, so we'll have to
go back to the town and give the
shopkeeper the diamond in exchange."

Elenna was kneeling beside him,
laughing as Silver licked her face.
Then, as if it came out of nowhere,
Tom saw the golden hilt of a sword
crack against the back of his friend's
head.

"Elenna!" he cried.

Elenna's laughter turned to a shout of agony. She collapsed, face down on the ground.

Tom looked up. A dazzle of sunlight almost blinded him for a moment. When his vision cleared, he recognised the tall woman with flowing black hair who was standing in front of him, her intense gaze fixed on him.

"Freya!" he exclaimed.

# CHAPTER TEN

# THE RIDDLE SOLVED

Tom stared at Velmal's companion. In one hand, Freya carried the golden rope, and in the other the sword that had struck Elenna. The sun shone on her suit of armour. It looked just like the magic suit of armour that Tom and his father Taladon had both worn. Why had Freya helped them out of the cavern, just to turn on them a moment later? Tom didn't understand.

"You?" he blurted out. Wizard Aduro and Taladon had both warned him not to fight with Freya, but he was so furious that he didn't care about their warning any more. "How dare you hurt Elenna!" he shouted.

"This is between you and me, Tom," Freya declared. "No one else."

Tom looked at Elenna. His friend was lying on her side on the ground, not moving. Silver stood over her, his teeth drawn back in a snarl.

"Stay with her, boy," Tom ordered. Scrambling to his feet, he slashed through the air with his sword. Freya dodged rapidly to one side, and the blade swung harmlessly past her. She smiled; Tom thought there was a hint of sadness in her face. Then she stepped forward into the fight, raising her glittering sword.

Tom blocked the blow and felt the force of it shiver down his arm. At once, Freya leapt back and aimed another blow at him. Tom was only just able to catch it on his shield. A moment later he had to jump over Freya's blade as she swept it around level with his knees.

*Freya's a good fighter,* he thought. *Really good! But I must win this battle!*

Fury still surged through Tom. Freya had hurt Elenna, just at their moment of triumph when they had freed Trema and escaped from the cavern. He wanted to see her defeated.

But Tom's injured hand was hurting badly, sending waves of pain up his arm. He was already tired from his struggle with Trema. His

heart was pumping and he could feel
sweat coursing down his back as he
hurled himself at Freya again and
again.

Freya didn't seem tired at all. She
moved swiftly and neatly, pressing
Tom back as her blade beat down on
his shield. It was all he could do to
defend himself.

At last Tom thought he saw a
chance – he stepped forward,
bringing his weapon around to catch
Freya's sword arm. Freya whirled to
one side; her blade slid down Tom's
own and she twisted it, throwing
Tom off balance.

Tom stumbled and fell. Lying helplessly on his back, he saw Freya standing over him, the tip of her sword poised over his heart. Her eyes were narrowed as she gazed down at him.

Tom gritted his teeth, waiting for the killing blow.

But Freya didn't move. Looking up at her, Tom saw that in her moment of victory, her eyes were brimming with tears.

Freya's hesitation was all Tom needed. Rolling away, he leapt to his feet, pushing Freya's blade aside with his own. *It's not over yet!*

As Tom brought his blade back around, its edge caught Freya's wrist. A shallow wound opened up and bright red drops of blood spattered to the ground. Dropping her sword, Freya cried out in pain as she grasped her injured wrist.

Tom stepped back, lowering his sword. He had won fairly, and he would gain nothing by killing Freya.

As he bent down to pick up Freya's sword, Tom felt a few drops of her blood fall onto his damaged hand. At

once the pain vanished. The swelling
subsided and the red colour faded.
Krabb's claw marks closed up and
shrank until they disappeared. Tom
stared disbelievingly at his trembling
fingers. Krabb's poison had been
cured; Tom's hand was healthy again!

At the same moment an angry cry
from Velmal echoed among the rocks.
Tom spun around, but the evil wizard
was nowhere to be seen.

"Too bad, Velmal!" Tom shouted
defiantly. "I've won, and my hand is
healed!"

Tom turned back to look at Freya.
She wouldn't meet his gaze and
lowered her head to stare at the
ground.

"What does this mean?" Tom asked,
but Freya didn't reply.

A moan from the ground nearby

made Tom turn around. Elenna was staggering to her feet, one hand rubbing the back of her head.

"Elenna, are you all right?" Tom asked anxiously.

"I think so," Elenna replied as she stumbled to Tom's side. Then she let out a gasp. "Tom! Your hand – it's healed! How did it happen?"

Tom shook his head, bewildered. He couldn't answer that question. The words of Velmal's riddle swirled around in his mind.

*Ichor Ofkin, Kin ichor…*

*Ofkin…ofkin…of kin…kin…*

*Kin means 'family',* Tom thought.

Red to red, life from death…

Tom turned back to Freya, willing her to look at him. After a long moment she raised her face and met his eyes. Gazing at her, Tom saw for the first time what he had missed.

*How could I have been such a fool for so long?*

"What is it?" Elenna tugged Tom's arm urgently. "What's going on?"

Tom raised his healed hand and pointed it at Freya. "She cured my poisoned hand," he said. "Velmal's riddle was telling me that the blood of someone in my family would return me to life."

"In your family…?" Elenna's voice was sharp with surprise.

Tom's mind swirled with confusion and disbelief. His Quest had just taken a whole new turn. And yet he had never been more sure of anything in his life.

"Elenna," he said. "Freya's my mother!"

Here's a sneak preview of Tom's
next exciting adventure!

Meet

# AMICTUS
# THE BUG QUEEN

Only Tom can free the Beasts from
Velmal's wicked enchantment...

# PROLOGUE

"By the Son of Gwildor!" Gil cursed, slicing his rusty machete through the undergrowth. "These roots are as thick as my wrist." The medicine man pushed through the brambles, grimacing as thorns scratched his cheeks.

The jungle was awash with searing colour. Gil's eyes watered at the scorching yellows, emerald greens and blood-red flowers. Even the tree trunks shone like copper. As he gazed at the top of the jungle canopy, a pair of birds soared above, their rainbow feathers glowing against the azure blue of the sky.

Gil dragged his canvas bag around his body and clamped it to his chest. His eyes darted from tree to tree as he stepped into the jungle. He wouldn't be the only person searching for Chulla roots, so he had to move quickly.

Anxiously, he shifted the machete in his hand. Trees and vines blotted out the sun, but even in the gloom, the vivid colours of the jungle shone brightly. Gil could hear himself panting for breath. Each gasp filled his lungs with warm, humid air.

Next time I'll send an assistant, he promised himself. If he found enough Chulla root today, he might finally be able to afford one! With a lighter heart, his pace picked up and soon Gil was darting through the trees, peering at the rich brown earth.

As he circled a tree trunk, he was forced to leap to one side. He'd just managed to avoid stumbling over a row of lilac-coloured eggs, their smooth shells pulsing with light against the dark jungle floor.

"How curious..." Gil murmured. He looked about, aware that whatever creature laid these eggs might be watching him. But there was no movement in the jungle.

He crept over to the eggs. The row stretched away into the forest – who knew how far they went? These could easily fetch... Gil smiled as he realised he couldn't begin to calculate their worth. How could he when he'd never seen eggs like these before?

"Priceless!" he gasped, extending a trembling hand to stroke the cool surface of a lilac shell. The colours shimmered as he lifted the egg, placing it carefully inside his canvas sack. He dropped his machete to reach for the next egg.

**Follow this Quest to the end in
AMICTUS THE BUG QUEEN.**

# Win an exclusive
# Beast Quest T-shirt and goody bag!

Tom has battled many fearsome Beasts and we want to know
which one is your favourite! Send us a drawing or painting of
your favourite Beast and tell us in 30 words why you think
it's the best.

Each month we will select **three** winners to receive
a Beast Quest T-shirt and goody bag!

Send your entry on a postcard to
**BEAST QUEST COMPETITION**
Orchard Books, 338 Euston Road, London NW1 3BH.

Australian readers should email:
childrens.books@hachette.com.au

New Zealand readers should write to:
Beast Quest Competition, PO Box 3255, Shortland St,
Auckland 1140, NZ or email: childrensbooks@hachette.co.nz

**Don't forget to include your name and address.
Only one entry per child.**

**Good luck!**

# Fight the Beasts,
# Fear the Magic

# www.beastquest.co.uk

Have you checked out the Beast Quest website?
It's the place to go for games, downloads, activities,
sneak previews and lots of fun!

You can read all about your favourite beasts,
download free screensavers and desktop wallpapers
for your computer, and even challenge your friends
to a Beast Tournament.

Sign up to the newsletter at www.beastquest.co.uk
to receive exclusive extra content and the
opportunity to enter special members-only
competitions. We'll send you up-to-date info on all
the Beast Quest books, including the next exciting
series which features four brand-new Beasts!

## Series 5
### BEAST QUEST

Tom must travel to Gwildor, Avantia's twin kingdom,
to free six new Beasts from an evil enchantment...

978 1 40830 437 2     978 1 40830 438 9     978 1 40830 439 6

978 1 40830 440 2     978 1 40830 441 9     978 1 40830 442 6

SPECIAL BUMPER EDITION!

978 1 40830 436 5

Can Tom rescue the
precious Cup of Life
from a deadly two-
headed demon?